For Simon

The illustrations for this book were prepared using gouache.

FIRST EDITION
1 3 5 7 9 10 8 6 4 2

Library of Congress Cataloging-in-Publication Data
Henley, Claire.
Joe's pool/Claire Henley ~ 1st ed.
p. cm.
Summary: Joe's pool is just the right size for one,
but he becomes dismayed when more and more people crowd in to join him.
ISBN 1-56282-431-7 (trade) ~ 1-56282-432-5 (lib. bdg.)
[1. Swimming pools ~ Fiction.] I. Title
PZ7.H3893Jo 1994 [E] ~ dc20 92-33946 CIP AC

Joe's Pool

Claire Henley

Hyperion Books for Children
New York

It was a very hot day.
But Joe didn't mind.
He had a brand-new wading pool.
It was bright blue with fish painted
on the bottom.

Joe put on his bathing suit ~ the one
with the big anchor sewn on the front.
He lay back in his pool and watered his
toes with his watering can.
Joe shut his eyes and thought to himself,
This pool is perfect for ONE.

"May I get in?" squeaked a voice in his ear.
Joe looked up and saw Jessica from next door.
She already had one foot in the pool.
"I suppose there's room for TWO," Joe sighed.

A wet tail slapped Joe in the face.
Scruffy dived into the pool without even
being invited.
He gulped some water, then shook himself
and sprayed Joe from top to bottom.
"This pool just isn't big enough for THREE,"
Joe mumbled.

"Any room for me?" boomed Bill the
deliveryman.
He leaped into the pool and poured water
over his face with Joe's watering can.
Joe thought Bill's feet smelled.
"It's too small for FOUR," Joe muttered.

"Oooh ... just what I need to cool my feet!" exclaimed Joe's teacher.
She put down her books, pulled off her shoes, and stepped in.
The pool was getting pretty full.
"It's very crowded with FIVE," Joe said, but not too loudly, because he was trying to be polite.

The paperboy arrived.
"Hi! May I join you?" he asked, and rolled up
his jeans and climbed in.
It was very noisy in Joe's pool.
"It's a tight squeeze for SIX!" shouted Joe.

"Looks like fun," laughed Joe's mom.
"I never thought you could fit so many people in your pool, Joe. May I see what it's like?"

Joe glared, but his mom got in anyway and started talking to his teacher.
"I can't move in here with SEVEN!" cried Joe.

"Hello, everyone!" called the
mailwoman.
"Have you got a letter for me?"
asked Joe.
But the mailwoman didn't answer.
She was too busy untying her shoes.
"It's too squashed for EIGHT!"
screamed Joe.

"Whew! Can I leave my groceries here in the shade?" puffed Mr. Fisher on his way back from town.
He hitched up his pants and pushed his way into the pool.
"It's full with NINE!" roared Joe.

q

The painter came down his ladder, hung up his paint can, pulled up his overalls, and squeezed in.
"There isn't enough room in this pool for TEN!" yelled Joe at the top of his voice.
But no one heard.
Joe was angry.

10

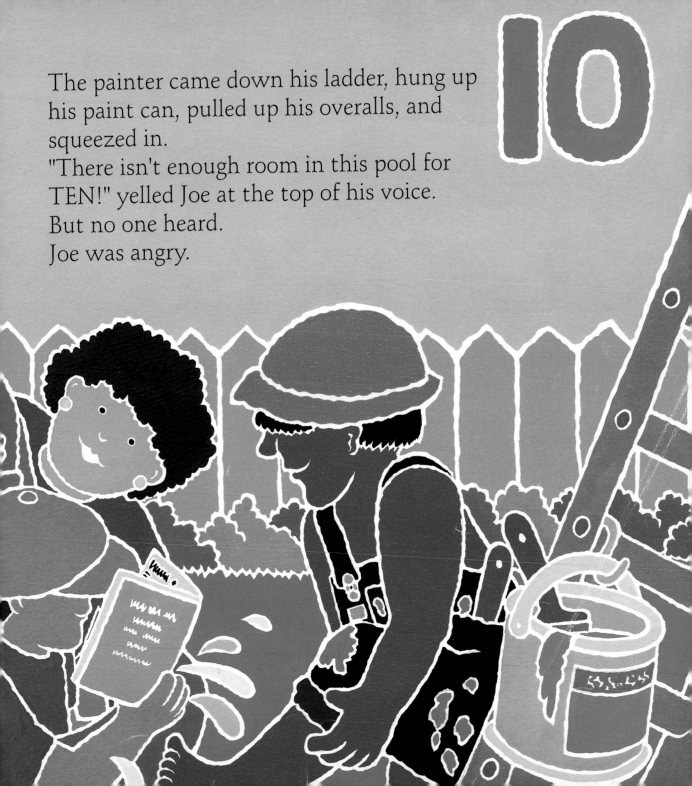

He heard the ice-cream man ringing his bell in the street.
Oh no, thought Joe.
Not another person who wants to get into my pool!

And then Joe thought of a plan to get every-one out of his pool once and for all ...
but before he could do anything, there was a lot of splashing and shouting ...
and Joe was left by himself.

It wasn't long before everyone came back carrying popsicles and ice-cream cones from the ice-cream man.

"Let's have an ice-cream party," said Joe's mom as she handed Joe a mouth-watering pink-and-green striped popsicle.

"Ah," Joe smiled. "This pool is perfect for me!"